GLASS TOWN

GLASS TOWN

by Michael Bedard

Paintings by Laura Fernandez and Rick Jacobson

Book Design: Andrew Smith
The text of this book is set in Adobe Garamond.
The paintings are rendered in oils on canvas.

*Stoddart Publishing gratefully acknowledges the support
of the Canada Council and the Ontario Arts Council in the
development of writing and publishing in Canada.*

First published in 1997 by
Stoddart Publishing Co. Limited
34 Lesmill Road
Toronto, Canada M3B 2T6
Phone (416) 445-3333
Fax (416) 445-5967
e-mail Customer.Service@ccmailgw.genpub.com

Published in the United States in 1997 by
Atheneum Books for Young Readers
1230 Avenue of the Americas
New York, New York 10020

Canadian Cataloguing in Publication Data
Bedard, Michael
Glass town
ISBN 0-7737-2997-6
1. Brontë, Emily, 1818-1848 – Juvenile fiction
I. Fernandez, Laura. II. Jacobson, Rick. III. Title

PS8553-E298G53   1997   jC813'.54   C96-931417-5
PZ7.B381798G1   1997

Printed and bound in Hong Kong

How little know we what we are,
How less what we may be.

ANNE'S DIARY PAPER, 1841

Foreword

In the year 1847 three books appeared within a space of months. They were *Jane Eyre* by Currer Bell, *Wuthering Heights* by Ellis Bell, and *Agnes Grey* by Acton Bell. It was not long before it was learned that the authors' names were pseudonyms, shielding behind them three sisters by the names of Charlotte, Emily, and Anne Brontë, who lived in the north of England in a remote village called Haworth.

Jane Eyre created an immediate sensation, for here was heard a new voice in fiction, the voice of a woman of passion and fire and fierce independence of spirit.

How three young women in such isolated circumstances could have produced such masterful work has always been a mystery. Something like a key to the mystery surfaced after their deaths, when among Charlotte Brontë's papers were discovered well over a hundred miniature books and magazines written in microscopic hand printing. At first they were considered a curiosity, but when finally they were deciphered it was discovered that they all formed part of a vast and intricate saga, begun in the year 1829 when the Brontës were children, and carried on well into their adult lives. It was here in the secret world they created among themselves that their imaginations had taken root and grown strong, in the soil of the city they called Glass Town.

1829

Haworth. A single, narrow street paved with cobblestone climbs the steep hill. To either side stand houses, roofed with stone. Night nears; the shutters are drawn closed.

At the top of the hill there stands a church; behind it, a churchyard thick with graves. Beyond that, on still higher ground, a solitary gray stone house. The graves sweep up to the garden wall.

This is the parsonage. It stands by itself between the little village and, rising in the distance, miles of empty moors. The wind off the moors makes a weird, unearthly moan.

The house seems empty—dark and still and lone. But on the upper floor there stands a little room. Four children work there now. One sits by the window. Two others play upon the floor. The fourth sits on a low stool by the door. Her name is Charlotte. Her writing box lies open on her lap and she is writing busily. She bends low to her work, for her eyes are weak.

Hear the scratch of the pen upon the page. Hear the wailing of the wind about the eaves. . . .

Twilight falls. The house is still. Downstairs, Papa is working on his sermon in the study. Tabby the servant is washing up after tea. As I write this I am sitting in the children's study on the upper floor of the parsonage, Haworth.

Anne, my youngest sister, is sitting on the floor, playing with the box of wooden soldiers which we call the Young Men. They belong to Branwell, our brother, who is sitting by her, busy with the little magazine we are making. We call it *The Young Men's Magazine*.

We write on scraps of paper no bigger than my palm, our words so small that only we can see.

We seek delight in secrecy.

At the window sits my other sister, Emily. Her writing desk is open on her lap. Beside her on the bed, Bewick's *History of British Birds* lies open. She has been copying the woodcut of the whinchat, a solitary bird that dwells upon the moors. It builds its nest at the roots of bushes or beneath stones, carefully concealing the entranceway.

Emily, too, is a solitary thing. She looks long, says little. Now she is looking at the sky. She reads the clouds as others read a book. She says a storm is on the way.

The wind blows wild about the house. Yet inside, stillness reigns. Aunt's room lies the other side of this wall. I imagine her sitting by the fire in her black silk gown, the remains of her tea on the table beside her, the *Methodist Monthly* open on her lap.

If we are quiet she will leave us be.

Anne has ranged the soldiers on the floor. They are in a sorry state now, scarred and wounded all. Yet how well I recall that day three years ago when Papa brought them brand-new back with him from Leeds.

It was night and we were all asleep, so he set the box by Branwell's bed. In the morning when he woke Branwell found them there and ran at once to show us.

Emily and I each took one up. Mine was the prettiest of all. "This is the Duke of Wellington," I said. Emily's had a grave-looking face, so she named him "Gravey." Then Anne came in and took one for herself. This one she called "Waiting Boy." Branwell chose last and said his would be "Bonaparte."

This was the origin of our first great play.

We acted out our play upon the moors; we whispered low at twilight here. From wood and paint we wove a web of dreams.

We woke a world, a world within, invisible to all eyes but our own.

We imagined marvelous adventures for our Young Men, daring exploits, battles, victories. The dead were always made alive again.

Weary of war, we had our soldiers turn explorers. We sent them sailing far across the sea in quest of unknown lands. We called the ship *Invincible*.

At first the sea was calm, the winds were fair. But one month out from land a storm approached. The wind rose and the sky grew dark. There was a fierce flash of lightning and a loud peal of thunder. The rain poured down in torrents and the gusts of wind were loud and terrible.

As last the storm ceased, but we found it had driven us quite off course, and we knew not where we were.

After many storms and months at sea, we sighted land. We sailed along the coast until we came upon a place where two great arms of land stretched out from shore and took the waters in their calm embrace.

We landed there, dropped anchor in a harbor still as glass, our battered ship at rest at last. . . .

Today we woke to the sound of Papa's pistol. It is his habit to sleep with it beneath his pillow and on waking to fire it out his window toward the church tower across the way. Thus begins our day.

Branwell sleeps with Papa in his room, Anne with Aunt, while Emily and I share the narrow bed in this narrow room between.

There was a damp chill to the air and the bare floor was cold underfoot. We keep neither carpets on the floor nor curtains on the windows, for Papa has a fear of fire. Nor do we wear cotton or linen, but rather silk or wool.

We dressed quickly. I made the bed, while Emily ran off to feed her pets.

I stood at the window. My view was this: a small yard fenced with stone, within its confines bushes, budding now, a square of grass, a gravel walk; beyond the wall, the churchyard, so thick with graves the wild grass scarce finds room to spring between. The flat black stones were slick with dew. A redbreast perched on one and sang its song.

Across the churchyard rose the gray tower of the church where Papa preaches, and beneath whose aisle my mother and two older sisters lie. Of Mother I have little memory. But of Maria and Elizabeth the memory is clear and keen.

In the distance the sun rose gloriously over the moors, chasing off the darkness, casting clouds aside. I felt its warm rays on my face through the glass.

I closed my eyes that I might see, and felt the vision's spell sweep over me.

Instantly I was away. The scene spread out before me. I saw the boat at anchor in the sapphire waters of the bay. I felt the radiant heat. I saw a land of vines and flowers and almond trees. I heard the scented wind among the leaves.

I looked upon a vast and fertile plain, bounded on the north by mist-enshrouded mountains, on the east by deep, impenetrable forests, on the west by burning deserts, on the south by the sea.

It was here we set about establishing a city. The splendid palaces, the mighty towers rose magically from the plain, reflected in the deep, still waters of the bay.

We called the city Glass Town.

After breakfast Emily and I brushed and dusted the sitting room and Papa's study. Apart from those few we keep in our room, what books we have are here. They sit upon the shelves beside the fire, so small, so still; yet within its covers each contains a world.

Those in Greek or Latin exceed our skill. But there are others there as well. The works of Walter Scott, for novels; for poets, Milton, Cowper, Southey, and the great Lord Byron. Papa puts no curbs upon our reading, and we devour all.

Emily ran her cloth along the spines, took this then that one down, like ripe fruit from the bough. She let the page fall open where it would, read a verse or two.

I dusted the pictures on the wall. I stood upon the chair and ran my cloth with care along the frames, cleared the veil of dust upon the glass, brought my eyes up close, and gazed in wonder on the world that opened there.

They are the work of Mr. Martin, marvels all. The mighty towers, the terraced walls of ancient cities; the skies a mass of seething clouds shot through with lightning, save for where the sun breaks through and bathes the scene in wondrous light.

I felt a fire kindled in my soul.

I saw the mighty towers of Glass Town rising from the plain, the walls and ramparts of tremendous height, the streets a quarter of a mile wide, lined with shops and buildings of wondrous design, their pillars gleaming pale as ice.

I saw the palaces and public buildings of radiant white marble and in their midst, the Tower of All Nations. What words can describe its splendor? Like the vast remains of a vanished world it stood in silent grandeur, rising above the clouds, seeking the acquaintance of the skies.

It was a bright and wondrous dream, an earthly paradise.

We heard the clack of wooden pattens in the passageway. Emily closed her book. My idle cloth went back to work. We turned from dreams to dust again.

Aunt stood in the doorway. "Whatever are you doing, Charlotte?" she asked when she saw me standing on the chair.

"Why dusting, Aunt," I said. She stood in her black silk dress, her purple shawl about her shoulders, her large lace cap upon her head. She goes about the house with wooden pattens strapped onto her shoes, to raise her feet above the damp stone floor. She has a dreadful fear of chill.

"It is time for your lessons," she said. Aunt keeps us strictly to the clock that stands upon the landing of the stairs. Order is her love.

She set us to our lessons in the parlor. Papa had laid them out. Questions from *Goldsmith's Grammar of Geography*, a spelling list, a piece of scripture to be had by heart.

Our hearts lay elsewhere. Emily sat at the window seat with her writing box and stared off at the dim, blue distant hills. She chafes at her studies like a chained thing, yearning to be free.

Anne studied her scripture dutifully. I sat with *Goldsmith's,* staring at the colored maps of distant lands, and dreamed. The steady *chip-chip* of the stonemason's hammer, the solemn tolling of the passing bell fell upon my ear. They became the bells of Glass Town, announcing the hour of noon, while high above the rest the great cathedral bell sent forth its mighty knell.

Papa taught Branwell in his study alone. He says he shows great promise. Branwell has never been to school. Emily and I were sent away to school once. Maria and Elizabeth were also there. It was a dark and dreadful place. Death brought us home.

Aunt took the morning sun in her room.

After lessons, we took a turn in the garden, arm in arm around the gravel path.

We wove a tale of Glass Town, whispering as we walked. Now I was the Duke of Wellington, Anne was Captain Ross, and Emily was Parry.

Aunt watched from her window up above, but knew nothing of our play.

Dinner was at two. We had boiled beef, turnips, potatoes, and apple pudding. Papa ate as always in his study; Aunt took a tray in her room.

We sat in the kitchen with Tabby. She has lived in Haworth all her life and has many a tale of times gone by, when restless spirits roamed the empty moors and fairies danced in rings on moonlit nights.

After dinner, Papa and Branwell left for Keighley, a small town four miles from here. They went for the newspapers and to visit Mr. Driver, the Haworth doctor. He lends us *Blackwoods Magazine*, the most able periodical there is.

We stayed behind and helped to tidy up, then Tabby said that we might go and play.

Out through the gate in the garden wall we ran, and down the little lane; past fence and field, till wall and fence and field all fell away, and empty moorland, wide and lone, spread far as eye could see. There seemed no one in the world but we.

The snow was all but gone, save for a few chill lingering islands scattered in the distance here and there, yielding to the sun. The thaw had filled the brooks; the sound of bounding water filled the air. The wind blew brisk and free. From rim to rolling rim of world the clouds went racing by.

Emily ran on ahead, hair flying in the wind. All her quiet fell away; she was wild and gay and full of glee, as playful as a pup—bounding forward, hastening back to urge us on, then off as quick again. She dwells within these walls with us, and yet her home lies there. She is a child of the moors, a friend of all things wild and free. She feeds on cloud and drinks the wind.

She took Anne by the hand and struck out from the path across the trackless heath, in search of grouse nests and early violets.

I followed after with uncertain step, up hill, down dale, till wearied of the game I sat down on a warm stone in the sun. The wind swept in warm gusts over the brown grass, shook the tender spires of green that grew among them. I closed my eyes and felt the warm sun on my face, and thought of Glass Town, glimmering in the heat.

The bliss was brief. The sun sank low; the wind rose in great swells with the falling light. It blew Emily and Anne back from their play. We hurried home along the path; our shadows stretched before us as we ran.

The clock upon the stair struck four. We hurried up to Aunt's room. There each day we sit and sew. The room is dim and close. A constant fire burns in the grate. Aunt sat in her straight-backed chair and complained of chill.

Anne worked on her sampler. Her small hands still lack skill. Emily works well. She has recently completed her sampler, a passage from Proverbs, the letters neat and straight and small. Today she hemmed a length of calico for pillow slips. I turned a piece of brown silk for a dress. Our clothes are in the fashion Aunt wore as a child.

Aunt says it is proper that women learn to sew. She sits close by the fire and watches all, her Indian workbox open at her side, her embroidery frame across her lap. She stoops to pluck a spool of gaily colored silk, cuts it short, threads her needle's narrow eye with skill.

On her shelves there lie some *Ladies Magazines*, with finely dressed ladies and tales of romance. There, too, are her *Methodist Magazines*. Her faith is cheerless, full of dread and fear. She strives to bend our will to this. But Emily will not be bent. A fire burns as constant in her eyes as in the grate. Aunt sees it there and says that she will come to ill.

I hold my work close and keep my stitches small.

Papa and Branwell returned in time for tea. We sat in the parlor and Papa read aloud from the papers and Branwell from the latest *Blackwoods Magazine*. And then the time was ours till sleep.

Now the night draws near, the room grows dim. We have no fire here. Branwell has just gone down and begged a candle from Tabby. We sit upon the floor about the flame; I, busy with this work, Branwell finishing our little magazine.

Anne has fetched her workbox. She threads her needle while Branwell takes the scissors out and trims an empty sugar bag into a cover for our magazine. Anne binds it with a stitch—and it is done.

He proudly shows it round. What strange delight it is to see this dream we dreamt now written down.

Our soldiers have become authors now. We dip our pens in dream. There will be books piled high upon the waiting shelves in Glass Town.

Soon the house will echo with the dismal sound of the clock striking seven and we shall be summoned off to bed. But first we shall lay the soldiers to sleep in their narrow box, and Branwell will pry the loose floorboard free, that we might hide this little work away.

There will be prayers in the parlor, then a candle will light our way up the shadowed stairs.

Anne will disappear behind Aunt's door, we behind ours, and Branwell will bear the candle into Papa's room, where he will read his *Blackwoods* quietly and listen for Papa's footsteps on the stairs.

Soon Papa too will come, pausing on the landing to wind the clock. He will go into his room, close his door, take his watch from his waistcoat and set it on the table by the bed, take his pistol from his pocket and slide it beneath his pillow. Then he will quench his candle, undress in the dark, and settle into bed.

And Emily and I will lie together in our narrow bed and listen, till the house grows still and all are laid asleep. And the moon will shed her silver light down on us here. And the night wind will rise and sweep in mighty swells down off the moors, and howl with such awful grandeur about the house that you would think to hear the voice of spirits in the storm.

And we will thrill to the wildness of the wind and in low voices we will weave a play.

The clock will sound the passing hour, our words grow spare, the silence spring between. Emily's eyes will droop, then close; her breath come calm and deep. And I will nestle close in the chill room and listen to her breathe. Then close my eyes and lay me on the wind, away to Glass Town and the world within.